The Primary Source Library of the Thirteen Colonies and the Lost Colony™

The Colony of New Jersey
A Primary Source History

Jake Miller

The Rosen Publishing Group's
PowerKids Press™
New York

Published in 2006 by The Rosen Publishing Group, Inc.
29 East 21st Street, New York, NY 10010

First Edition

Editor: Jennifer Way
Book Design: Ginny Chu
Photo Researcher: Cindy Reiman

Photo Credits: Cover and title page © Delaware Art Museum, Wilmington, USA, Howard Pyle Collection/Bridgeman Art Library; p. 4 © Corbis; p. 4 (inset) © Getty Images; p. 6 Library of Congress Geography and Map Division; p. 6 (inset) Library of Congress Prints and Photographs Division HABS, NJ, 8-SWEBO.V, 6-1; p. 8 I. N. Phelps Stokes Collection, Miriam and Ira D. Wallach Division of Art, Prints and Photographs, The New York Public Library, Astor, Lenox and Tilden Foundations; p. 8 (inset) Victoria & Albert Museum, London/Art Resource, NY; p. 10 © Stapleton Collection/Corbis; pp. 10 (inset), 14 (inset) New Jersey State Archives, Department of State; p. 12 Library of Congress Rare Book and Special Collections Division; p. 12 (inset) Philip Mould, Historical Portraits Ltd., London, UK/Bridgeman Art Library; p. 14 Map Division, The New York Public Library, Astor, Lenox and Tilden Foundations; p. 16 Picture Collection, The Branch Libraries, The New York Public Library, Astor, Lenox and Tilden Foundations; p. 16 (inset) The New York Public Library/Art Resource, NY; p. 18 Art Resource, NY; p. 18 (inset) Independence National Historical Park; p. 20 Culver Pictures; p. 20 (inset) © Francis G. Mayer/Corbis

Library of Congress Cataloging-in-Publication Data

Miller, Jake, 1969–
    The colony of New Jersey : a primary source history / Jake Miller.— 1st ed.
        p. cm. — (The primary source library of the thirteen colonies and the Lost Colony)
    Includes bibliographical references and index.
    ISBN 1-4042-3031-9 (library binding)
    1. New Jersey—History—Colonial period, ca. 1600–1775—Juvenile literature. 2. New Jersey—History—1775–1865—Juvenile literature. I. Title.

F137.M54 2006
974.9'02—dc22
                                                                    2004025428

Manufactured in the United States of America

Contents

This picture shows Henry Hudson's 1609 journey along the East Coast. His boat, in the background, was called the Half Moon. Inset: Henry Hudson lived from about 1575 until 1611. Hudson wanted to find a route from Europe to Asia. Although he did not find one, his trips added to the knowledge of North America's coast.

Explorers and Settlers

Henry Hudson was one of the first Europeans to see the land that became New Jersey. Hudson was an Englishman sailing for the Netherlands' Dutch East India Company. In 1609, he explored, or traveled to, the New Jersey coast. He also sailed up a river that was later named for him, the Hudson River.

Soon after Hudson explored the land, other explorers, traders, and settlers began to come from Europe. In the 1630s, the Netherlands, Sweden, and England all sent colonists to the land that is now New Jersey. Most of these colonists were farmers. Long before those colonists arrived, though, there were already Native American people living there. The Delaware, Raritan, Hackensack, Wappinger, and other groups of **Algonquin** peoples had lived there for many years.

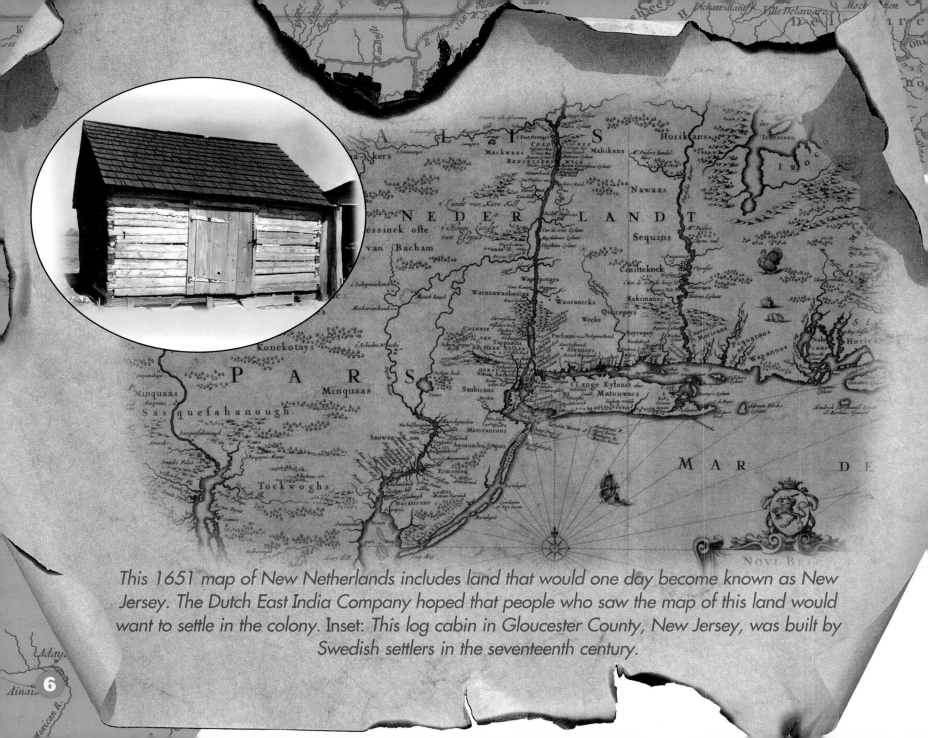

This 1651 map of New Netherlands includes land that would one day become known as New Jersey. The Dutch East India Company hoped that people who saw the map of this land would want to settle in the colony. Inset: This log cabin in Gloucester County, New Jersey, was built by Swedish settlers in the seventeenth century.

6

New Netherlands

The first settlements in New Jersey were part of a colony of the Dutch East India Company called New Netherlands. This colony included the lands that became parts of New Jersey, New York, and Delaware. The first lasting settlement in New Jersey was Bergen, now Jersey City, in 1660.

In the early 1600s, Britain had North American colonies in New England and in the Chesapeake Bay. The British had earlier claimed North American lands that lay between Canada and Florida, which included New Netherlands. Britain did not want to fight the Dutch over New Netherlands but they soon took control of it.

New Sweden
The earliest European settlers in southern New Jersey were part of a Swedish colony known as New Sweden. The Swedes brought settlers from other countries, such as Finland. The Dutch conquered New Sweden in 1655 and made it part of New Netherlands.

This 1664 map of New Amsterdam is one of the earliest maps of the area. Some of New Amsterdam's forts are shown, in addition to the lakes, rivers, and hills that are often included on maps. Inset: King Charles II lived from 1630 until 1685.

The English Province of New Jersey

Charles II, king of England, wanted the lands of New Amsterdam more than he wanted peace with the Dutch. On September 8, 1664, English warships sailed into New Amsterdam, New Netherlands' capital. The Dutch knew they could not beat the British and gave up the colony without a fight.

King Charles gave New Amsterdam, which included parts of New Jersey, to his brother James, the Duke of York. The area was renamed New York in his honor. James split off a small piece of land between the Hudson and Delaware rivers and gave it to Sir George Carteret and Sir John Berkeley in 1664. They were friends with the Duke of York and King Charles. This new colony was named the **province** of New Jersey after Carteret's home, the Isle of Jersey in England.

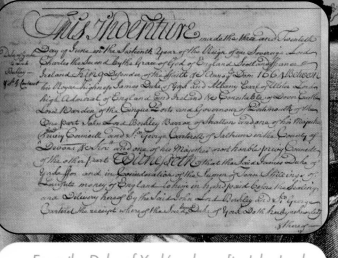

This Indenture made the [illegible] and Twentieth Day of June in the Sixteenth Year of the Reign of our Soveraign Lord Charles the Second by the Grace of God of England Scotland France and Ireland King Defender of the Faith &c Anno Dm 166 [illegible] Between his Royal highness James Duke of York and Albany Earl of Ulster Lord high Admiral of England and Ireland &c Constable of Dover Castle Lord Warden of the Cinque Ports and Governour of Portsmouth of the One part John Lord Berkley Barron of Stratton and one of his Majesties privy Councell and Sr George Carteret of Saltrum in the County of Devon Knight and one of his Majesties most honble privy Councell of the other part Witness that the Said James Duke of York for and in Consideration of the Summe of Tenn Shillings of [illegible] [illegible] money of England to him in hand paid before the Sealing and Delivery hereof by the Said John Lord Berkley and Sr George Carteret the receipt whereof the Said Duke of York Doth hereby acknowledge thereof...

From the Duke of York's release [to John Lord Berkley, and Sir George Carteret]

"James Duke of York, doth hereby acknowledge... and confirm unto the said John Lord Berkley and Sir John Carteret, their heirs and assigns for ever, all that tract of land . . . hereafter to be called by the name or names of New Caeserea or New Jersey."

The above passage says that James, the Duke of York, is giving Berkeley and Carteret a piece of his land. This land is to be named either New Caeserea or New Jersey. Other parts of the release describe in detail the borders of the land James is granting the men.

The picture above shows a Quaker church service, called a meeting. The Quaker church was begun in the mid-1600s by an Englishman named George Fox. Many Quakers moved to the colonies, including New Jersey, for religious freedom. Inset: *The Duke of York's 1664 release granted New Jersey to Berkeley and Carteret. Berkeley sold his share of the land in 1674.*

Two Jersey Colonies

In 1674, Berkeley sold his share of New Jersey to two English **Quakers**. One of these owners was Edward Billinge, who sold his share in 1676. This land became known as West Jersey. Carteret's share became known as East Jersey.

East Jersey was settled by many groups, including Dutch, Swedish, Finnish, and Scottish. Some of the biggest settlements were made up of Puritans who came from Massachusetts and Connecticut in the 1670s. The Puritans founded the cities of Newark and Elizabethtown, which is now known as Elizabeth.

West Jersey was settled by Quakers. They wanted a place where they could live according to their beliefs. One of the **investors** who had bought West Jersey from Billinge was a Quaker named William Penn.

This picture shows New Jersey farmland. Farmers and landlords often did not agree about land ownership and to whom taxes were to be paid. This problem led to fighting. Inset: Queen Anne brought together the two Jerseys in 1702. New Jersey became one of the 13 British colonies on North America's East Coast.

Bringing the Two Jerseys Together

For many years the people who controlled East Jersey and West Jersey had trouble collecting rent and taxes from their colonists. The land had changed ownership so many times that people were uncertain about who owned the land. They were not sure who was allowed to collect rent and taxes. The landlords and rulers all had different ideas about who owned the land. Some even sold land that belonged to other people.

Finally, in 1702, the power to govern the two Jerseys was given back to Britain. Queen Anne brought together the two Jerseys to make New Jersey, to be run by the governor of New York. The landlords hoped that in the new royal colony, governed directly by the Crown, the farmers would be easier to control. In 1738, New Jersey was granted its own governor.

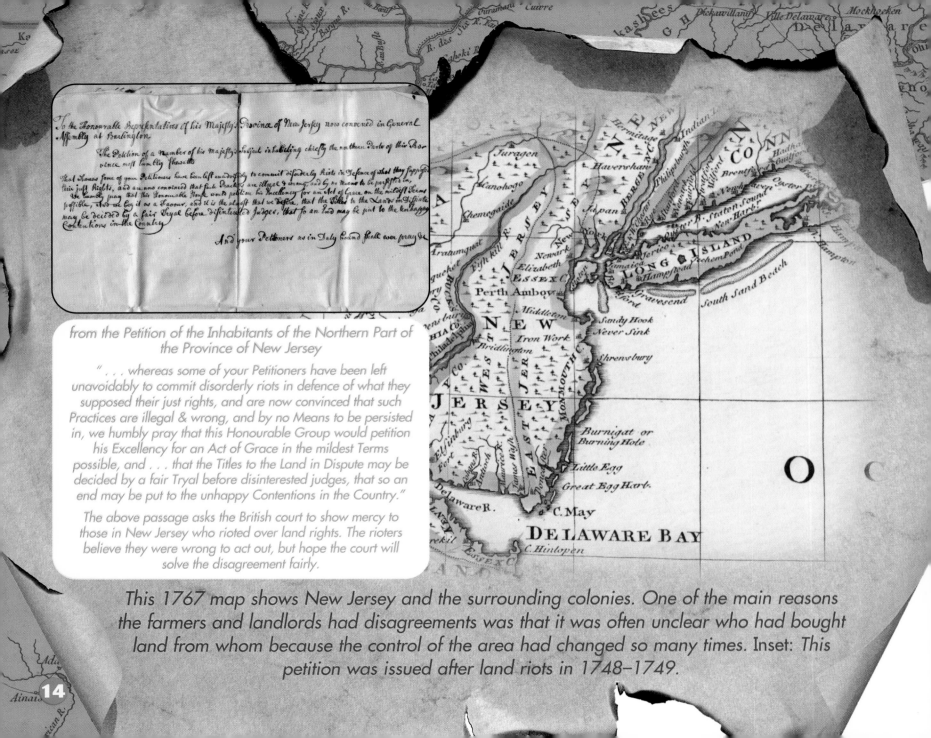

from the Petition of the Inhabitants of the Northern Part of the Province of New Jersey

" . . . whereas some of your Petitioners have been left unavoidably to commit disorderly riots in defence of what they supposed their just rights, and are now convinced that such Practices are illegal & wrong, and by no Means to be persisted in, we humbly pray that this Honourable Group would petition his Excellency for an Act of Grace in the mildest Terms possible, and . . . that the Titles to the Land in Dispute may be decided by a fair Tryal before disinterested judges, that so an end may be put to the unhappy Contentions in the Country."

The above passage asks the British court to show mercy to those in New Jersey who rioted over land rights. The rioters believe they were wrong to act out, but hope the court will solve the disagreement fairly.

This 1767 map shows New Jersey and the surrounding colonies. One of the main reasons the farmers and landlords had disagreements was that it was often unclear who had bought land from whom because the control of the area had changed so many times. Inset: This petition was issued after land riots in 1748–1749.

Fighting over Land Rights and Rent

Joining New Jersey into a single colony did not fix anything. The uncertainty over land rights and rent continued into the 1740s, when fighting between farmers and landlords broke out.

An example of these fights happened in 1745. A farmer named Samuel Baldwin was arrested for not paying his rent. He claimed that he had bought the land from its Native American owners and so should not have to pay rent. When he was arrested, an angry crowd of farmers broke him out of jail. Two of the men who freed Baldwin were arrested, and hundreds of angry settlers gathered around the jail. The guards at the jail tried to stop the crowd, but some members of the crowd started to beat the guards. The guards fought back, and people on both sides were hurt.

The colonists in this picture are campaigning against the Stamp Act. In Britain men elected members of Parliament, who represented the voters when they decided on laws and taxes. Colonists did not elect members of Parliament but were expected to follow its laws and pay its taxes. Inset: George III lived from 1738 until 1820.

New Jersey Objects to Unfair Taxes

After the British fought the costly **French and Indian War**, **Parliament** and King George III wanted the colonies to help pay for the war, which had been fought in North America. Parliament passed new taxes on the colonies. The colonists did not have any **representation** in Parliament, which they believed was unfair.

One of the least popular new taxes was the Stamp Act, which taxed paper products. In October 1765, leaders from nine colonies met in New York at the Stamp Act Congress. New Jersey's representatives were Joseph Borden, Hendrick Fisher, and Robert Ogden. Congress sent the king a letter called the Declaration of Rights and Grievances, which explained why they thought the tax was unfair. The British ended the Stamp Act, but that did not end the problems between Britain and the colonies.

The picture above shows men on their way to the First Continental Congress in Philadelphia, Pennsylvania. Inset: John Witherspoon, who signed the Declaration of Independence, was a minister and the president of the College of New Jersey.

New Jersey at the Continental Congress

When the protests against the British began, the colonists only wanted fair treatment. Leaders from the 13 colonies met at the Continental Congress in September 1774, in Philadelphia, Pennsylvania. They talked about working out their problems with Britain. The representatives from New Jersey were James Kinsey, William Livingston, Stephen Crane, John Hart, and Richard Smith. The problems continued to worsen, and the **American Revolution** broke out in April 1775.

In July 1776, the Congress met again. One of New Jersey's representatives was John Witherspoon. On July 4, Congress signed the **Declaration of Independence**. The colonies also agreed to work together to fight the British and to govern themselves under the **Articles of Confederation**.

The above picture shows the Battle of Trenton, in New Jersey, which helped the Continental army believe they could win more battles. Inset: George Washington was the commander of the Continental army and was later the first president of the United States.

The American Revolution in New Jersey

By December 1776, the **Continental army** commander George Washington led his men across New Jersey to the far side of the Delaware River in Pennsylvania. On December 25, the **Hessian** troops had stopped fighting to observe the Christmas holiday. While the Hessians celebrated, George Washington slipped across the half-frozen Delaware River with 2,400 troops. They crossed the river in boats and then marched to Trenton to take the Hessians by surprise. Four days later Washington and his men took the city of Trenton, New Jersey.

The Battle of Trenton was a great success for the Continental army. It gave them hope that they could beat the British. The war was just beginning. Fighting lasted until 1781. The war officially ended in 1783 with the signing of the Treaty of Paris.

New Jersey Joins a New Nation

After the Revolution the nation needed to create a new government because the Articles were too weak to govern the country. In 1787, the states held the Constitutional Convention to plan the new government. The states disagreed about how the states' number of representatives would be decided. In one plan representation was based on a state's population. This meant that states with large populations would have more representatives than would small states, such as New Jersey. The leaders from small states felt that this was unfair. William Patterson of New Jersey suggested a plan that would give small states equal representation. Later a compromise, or agreement, satisfied both large and small states. New Jersey approved the **Constitution** on December 18, 1787, and became the third state.

Glossary

Algonquin (al-GON-kwin) Having to do with a group of Native Americans living in eastern North America.

American Revolution (uh-MER-uh-ken reh-vuh-LOO-shun) Battles that soldiers from the colonies fought against Britain for freedom, from 1775 to 1783.

Articles of Confederation (AR-tih-kulz UV kun-feh-deh-RAY-shun) The laws that governed the United States before the Constitution was created.

Constitution (kon-stih-TOO-shun) The basic rules by which the United States is governed.

Continental army (kon-tih-NEN-tul AR-mee) The army of patriots created in 1775.

Declaration of Independence (deh-kluh-RAY-shun UV in-duh-PEN-dints) A paper signed July 4, 1776, stating that the American colonies were free from British rule.

French and Indian War (FRENCH AND IN-dee-yun WOR) The battles fought between 1754 and 1763 by England, France, and Native Americans for control of North America.

Hessian (HEH-shen) Having to do with the German soldiers who were paid to fight for the British during the American Revolution.

investors (in-VES-turz) People who give money for something they hope will bring them more money later.

Parliament (PAR-lih-mint) The group in Great Britain that makes that country's laws.

province (PRAH-vins) A country that is run by another country.

Quakers (KWAY-kurz) People who belong to a faith that believes in equality for all people, strong families and communities, and peace.

representation (reh-prih-zen-TAY-shun) The act of speaking on behalf of a person or a group of people.

Index

Primary Sources

Page 6. Map of East Coast of North America (detail). Circa 1651, Claes Janszoon Visscher, Library of Congress Geography and Map Division. **Page 8.** Earliest English Map of New Jersey. 1664, I. N. Phelps Stokes Collection, Miriam and Ira D. Wallach Division of Art, Prints and Photographs, The New York Public Library, Astor, Lenox and Tilden Foundations. **Page 8. Inset.** *Charles II* (detail). Etching, 17th century, William I. Faithorne, Victoria & Albert Museum, London, United Kingdom. **Page 10.** *The Quakers Meeting* (detail). Engraving, circa 1640 after Maarteen van Heemskerck, Stapleton Collection. **Page 10. Inset.** The Duke of York's Release to John Lord Berkeley, and Sir George Carteret. June 24, 1664, New Jersey State Archives. **Page 12.** *A View at Pahaquarric, Sussex County, New Jersey*. Etching, 1794, John Scoles (engraver), Jacob Hoffman (sketch), Library of Congress Rare Book and Special Collections Division, Washington D.C. Page 12. **Inset.** *Queen Anne* (detail). Oil-on-canvas painting, circa 18th century, Michael Dahl, Philip Mould, Historical Portraits Ltd., London, United Kingdom. **Page 14.** Map (detail). Engraving, 1747, Emanuel Bowen, New York Public Library. **Page 16.** *The stamp riots in New York*. Black and white print, 1765, New York Public Library. **Page 16. Inset.** *George III* (detail). Mezzotint, 18th century, Richard Houston, New York Public Library. **Page 18. Inset.** *John Witherspoon* (detail). Painting, 1783–1784, Charles Wilson Peale, Independence National Historical Park, Philadelphia, Pennsylvania. **Page 20. Inset.** *George Washington* (detail). Painting, circa 1795–1800, Gilbert Stuart.

Web Sites

Due to the changing nature of Internet links, PowerKids Press has developed an online list of Web sites related to the subject of this book. This site is updated regularly. Please use this link to access the list:
www.powerkidslinks.com/pstclc/newjers/